OTHER DELL YEARLING BOOKS YOU WILL ENJOY

DELL YEARLING BOOKS are designed especially to entertain and enlighten young people. Patricia Reilly Giff, consultant to this series, received her bachelor's degree from Marymount College and a master's degree in history from St. John's University. She holds a Professional Diploma in Reading and a Doctorate of Humane Letters from Hofstra University. She was a teacher and reading consultant for many years, and is the author of numerous books for young readers.

THE HAUNTED HOUSE

by Peggy Parish

illustrated by Paul Frame

A Dell Yearling Book

Published by
Dell Yearling
an imprint of
Random House Children's Books
a division of Random House, Inc.
New York

Visit us on the Web! www.randomhouse.com/kids

Educators and librarians, for a variety of teaching tools, visit us at
www.randomhouse.com/teachers

ISBN: 0-440-43459-9

Reprinted by arrangement with Simon and Schuster Children's Publishing

Printed in the United States of America

February 1981

40 39 38 37

OPM

For Debby, Georgia Ann,
Nola Beth, and Dan Smith

Contents

1.
A Big Surprise

"Home!" shouted Jed.

"Milk and cookies!" shouted Bill.

Liza ran to the front door.

"That's funny," she said. "The door is locked. Mom didn't say anything about going out, did she?"

"Not to me," said Bill. "Ring the bell. Maybe the door just slammed shut."

Liza rang the bell, but there was no answer.

"Just our luck," said Bill, "and I could almost taste milk and cookies. Maybe we could go in through a window."

"Mom will probably be here in a few minutes," said Jed. "Your stomach can wait."

The three children sat down on the steps.

A few minutes later Liza said, "Here's the car now. And Dad's with Mom. I wonder if anything is wrong."

Mrs. Roberts got out of the car. She said, "Children, I'm sorry. I was sure I would be back before you got home."

"Where have you been?" asked Bill.

"Buying a house," said Mr. Roberts.

"Buying a house!" said the children.

"Yes, we just bought the most marvelous place," said Mrs. Roberts. "It's just what you children wanted, a house with lots of woods."

"Hurray!" shouted the children.

"Do we know the house?" asked Liza.

"I think so," said Dad. "It's the old Blake place."

"The haunted house!" said the children.

"Oh, no!" said Liza. "You can't do that to us. I won't live in a haunted house."

"Now just a minute, Liza," said Dad. "It's

true people call it that, but there's never been any proof of it. Any house that stays vacant for a long time is likely to gain that reputation."

"Dad, why did no one live there?" asked Jed.

"Because it was haunted, stupid," said Bill. "Nobody wants to live in a haunted house."

"The real reason," said Dad, "was a legal tangle which would not permit the house to be sold or rented. But that's been cleared up."

"Jack Hobbs has been the caretaker," said Mom, "so the place is in quite good condition. You children are going to love it."

"No, I'm not!" said Liza. "I'll lose all my friends. Nobody will come to see me in a haunted house."

"Is that a promise?" said Bill. "No more giggling girls! Let's move today."

4

"And just think," said Jed, "we can have Halloween all year round with real live ghosts."

"Oh, you're both mean!" screamed Liza. "You're trying to scare me."

"Don't worry, Liza," said Bill. "Your screams would unhaunt any house. No respectable ghost could stand it."

"Liza," said Dad, "you're being silly. You know there's no such thing as a ghost."

But Liza stamped out of the room. Seconds later they heard the door to her room slam.

"She's really mad," said Dad.

"She'll get over it," said Bill. "Dad, could it have been the caretaker who haunted the house? You know, just to keep people away?"

"No," said Dad. "The first two caretakers lived in the house, but each of them left because they said they heard strange noises there. Then Jack Hobbs took over, but he never lived in the house. He had his own place. I think it was because of the first caretakers that the house began to be called haunted. Then when it stayed empty the stories grew."

"Do you think we should take the house?" asked Bill. "I love mysteries, but I don't know about tangling with a ghost."

"You're as bad as Liza," said Dad. "You just wait. You're going to love it as much as Mom and I do."

"When are we going to move?" asked Jed.

"The first of the month," said Dad.

"The first of the month!" said Bill. "That's just a few days away."

"That's right," said Mom, "and it means work for all of us. I want you children to sort through your things and get rid of all you no longer use."

"Get rid of!" said Bill. "I thought we were moving so we would have more space."

"True," said Mom. "But knowing you children there will never be enough space for all you collect."

"Oh, all right," said Bill. "We'll start tomorrow."

Liza came back in the room. She was crying.

"Why the tears?" asked Mom.

"Oh, Mom!" said Liza. "I just realized that if we move Mary and Jimmy won't be our next-door neighbors anymore."

"That's right!" said Bill. "We've lived next door to Mary and Jimmy all our lives. Why, they're our very best friends."

"Don't worry about it," said Dad. "You can have Mary and Jimmy out to visit."

"But it won't be the same," said Liza.

"Do we have to move, Dad?" asked Bill.

"Yes, we're going to move," said Dad. "And I'll bet all three of you are going to love it."

But that night all three children went to bed unhappy about the move.

2.
The New House

The next morning Liza was very quiet as she walked to school with Bill and Jed.

"Cheer up, Liza," said Jed. "It may not be too bad."

"Are you fellows going to tell?" asked Liza.

"Tell what?" said Bill.

"About the new house," said Liza.

"Of course," said Bill. "It will make celebrities of us."

"Don't you want to tell?" asked Jed.

"I'm just not ready to talk about it yet," said Liza.

"Maybe Liza's right," said Jed. "Maybe we shouldn't."

"Why not?" said Bill. "We've got big news and I'm all for telling it. Not everybody gets to live in a haunted house."

"But everybody will ask questions and we can't answer them," said Jed. "Remember, we haven't even been in the place. We'll feel dumb when we don't know anything to tell them."

"Yeah," said Bill. "I guess I would feel pretty stupid having to say 'I don't know' all the time. Let's not tell."

"Agreed," said Jed. "Okay, Liza?"

"Agreed," said Liza.

When the children got home from school Mom was waiting on the porch.

"There you are," she said. "I was hoping you would come straight home."

"What's the rush, Mom?" asked Jed. "Is something wrong?"

"Oh, no," said Mom. "But we have a cleaning crew working in the new house. I want to be sure everything is done properly. And I'm sure you three want to see the place. So get yourselves a quick snack and we'll go over there."

The children went to the kitchen.

"Things sure are moving fast," said Bill.

"Too fast for me," said Liza.

"Oh, I don't know," said Jed. "I'm beginning to get kind of excited about it all."

"Come to think of it," said Bill, "so am I."

The children ate their snack and rushed back to their mother.

"That was quick," said Mom. "Hop into the car."

As they were riding along Liza said, "Mom, how will we ever get to school? We sure can't walk."

"Don't worry," said Mom. "There's bus service. Your father has already checked that."

"That will be the life," said Bill. "I hope it's door-to-door service."

"It is," said Mom.

"This moving has its good points after all," said Jed.

"I think you will like the house," said Mom, "especially when you see the nice basement it has."

Mom turned into a long driveway.

"I never saw the house close up," said Jed. "It sure is sprawly."

"Now," said Mom, "I'm going to leave you

children to explore as you will. Just stay out of the way of the cleaning people."

The children took a good long look at the house.

"Our very own haunted house," said Bill.

"Who's supposed to haunt it?" asked Jed.

"Gee," said Bill, "I never thought of that. I mean that it had to be somebody. I thought it was just a ghost."

"It doesn't look haunted to me," said Liza. "It looks just like an ordinary house."

"Time will tell," said Bill. "Anyway, let's go in. What are we waiting for?"

Inside it was all confusion. The cleaning people were everywhere.

"Ugh," said Bill. "I can't stand this. Let's explore outside."

"But I want to see my room," said Liza.

"I forgot that," said Bill. "Hey, Mom!"

"Right here," answered Mom.

"Where do we sleep?" asked Bill.

"I'll show you," said Mom. "Come along."

"This house goes on and on," said Bill.

"You children will have to make a decision about rooms," said Mom. "Jed and Bill can have this room and Liza can have the one next to it, or if you want separate rooms there's an extra one upstairs next to ours. But that's your decision to make."

The children looked at one another. Then slowly they shook their heads.

"We'll stick together," said Jed.

Mom laughed and said, "I thought you would say that."

"Okay," said Jed. "We've seen our rooms. Now let's go look at the basement."

"All right," said Bill. "Then we'll go outside and explore."

"Come back in an hour or so," said Mom. "I do have to get home and make some dinner for us."

"Yeah, man," said Bill. "Haunted house or not, we've still got to eat."

"Don't worry, Mom," said Jed. "Bill will get us back in plenty of time."

3.
In the News

That night at supper everybody wanted to talk at once.

"Dad," said Jed, "that place is really neat. It's even better than at Grandpa's."

"I never thought I'd hear you say that," said Dad.

"And, Dad," said Bill, "we found just the

right tree for a tree house. We never got one built last summer, but this is a better tree than the one at Grandpa's."

"Better let me check it before you begin," said Dad. "Let's make sure it is a safe tree."

"Okay," said Jed.

"I forgot to look," said Liza. "Does the house have an attic? I've always wanted to live in a house with an attic."

"It has a real old-fashioned attic," said Dad.

"And one that is full of junk," said Mom. "That will be a rainy-day job for you children."

"You mean stuff was left in it?" asked Bill.

"Yes," said Dad. "We said we would be responsible for cleaning it up."

"Maybe we'll find something valuable," said Jed.

"I doubt it," said Mom. "But then you never can tell about old places like that."

"I wish moving day was tomorrow," said Bill.

"Don't worry," said Mom. "It will come soon enough."

"You children were so full of talk I forgot to tell you the big news," said Dad.

"Big news!" said Liza. "What big news?"

"We made the paper today," said Dad. "There's a piece in the afternoon edition about our buying the house."

"Yipes!" said Bill. "Where's the paper?"

All three children tore away from the table.

"Bring it in here," said Mom. "I want to hear it, too."

Jed reached the paper first.

"Look," he said. "Here it is on the front page, 'Haunted House Has New Owners.' "

"That's us," said Bill.

"Do hush, Bill," said Liza. "Hurry up, Jed."

The children went back to the dining room.

"You read it, Jed," said Mom.

"Okay, here goes," said Jed. " 'The "haunted house," which has been vacant for many years, has new owners. The Jack Roberts family has bought the old Blake place.

" 'The house was built in 1920 by John Blake. He lived in it until his death ten years ago. Since that time, because of legal complications, the house has remained vacant. Caretakers refused to live in it. They say John Blake comes back at night.

" 'Perhaps the Robertses will clear up this mystery. We wish them luck in their new venture.' "

"That makes me feel all creepy," said Liza.

"Anyway, we know who is supposed to haunt the house," said Bill.

"I wonder why John Blake comes back," said Jed.

"Maybe he left a buried treasure or something," said Bill.

"Why couldn't we have just an ordinary house?" asked Liza.

"Pooh!" said Bill. "That would be no fun. Anybody can have an ordinary house. Give me a good old haunted one anytime."

"Mom!" said Jed. "I just realized we start our spring vacation at the same time as we move."

"I know," said Mom. "And I'm delighted. I'm going to need all the help I can get."

Liza was very quiet.

"What happened to you, Liza?" asked Dad. "You haven't said anything for at least two minutes."

"Do you really think my friends will come to see me in a haunted house?" asked Liza.

"You just wait," said Dad. "They'll be begging for invitations."

"Sure," said Mom. "And when we get settled you children can have a party and invite all your friends to see a real haunted house."

"That will be neat," said Jed.

"Okay," said Dad, "off to bed with you. Tomorrow is another school day."

4.
Moving Day

The next few days were busy ones. The movers brought over packing boxes, and Liza, Jed, and Bill were responsible for packing their own things. They had to make up their minds about what to throw away and what to keep.

Finally moving day came. The whole

family was up and waiting when the van arrived.

When the van was loaded, Mom said, "All right, children, we'll go ahead so we can tell them where to put things."

Everybody piled into the car.

"This just doesn't seem real," said Liza. "We're leaving the house we've lived in all our lives."

"Up and on to better things," said Dad.

"But I'm not sure it's better," said Liza. "I already feel homesick for my old room."

"That's all right," said Mom. "To tell the truth, I feel a little bit that way myself. But I'm sure we'll both get over it as soon as we get the new house fixed up."

"Ah, girls," said Bill. "You never are sure of what you want."

"But that's a fact of life," said Dad. "We just have to take them as they are."

"Yeah, I guess you're right," said Bill.

After that everybody was quiet until they reached their new home. The moving van wasn't far behind them.

"Now you children stay out of the way until they get the furniture unloaded," said Dad. "Then we'll need you to pitch in."

"That's right," said Mom. "You're responsible for doing your own rooms."

"Okay," said Jed. "We'll stay outside until the moving men have finished."

The children watched the movers carry in the furniture. As soon as they had finished the children went to their rooms and began to unpack their things. Finally that afternoon Bill said, "That's enough. I've got to take a break."

"I'm with you on that," said Jed. "Let's get Liza and go to the woods."

"Good idea," said Bill.

Liza was ready to stop, too. She said, "I've

never worked that hard in one day. What are we going to do?"

"Go to the woods," said Bill.

The children went outside. Dad was there.

"We've had enough of working," said Jed. "Is it all right if we go to the woods?"

"Sure," said Dad. "I feel the same way."

"Then would you go with us and check our tree for the tree house?" asked Bill.

"All right," said Dad. "I can show you the boundary line for our woods, too."

"Boundary line!" said Jed. "I thought we owned all of the woods."

"Oh, no," said Dad. "We only own half of them."

Jed and Bill ran ahead to the woods. But Liza held her father's hand and skipped along beside him.

"Okay, Dad," said Jed. "This is it."

"It's a nice one, too," said Dad.

Dad went around testing the limbs. Then he said, "This is a good tree for a tree house."

"Yippee!" said Bill.

"Now where is the boundary line, Dad?" asked Jed.

"Back this way," said Dad. They walked through the woods. Finally they came to a fence.

"Is this it?" asked Bill.

"Yes," said Dad. "We own the land up to the fence."

"Who owns the rest?" asked Jed.

"Mr. Dan Coleman," said Dad.

On the way back home Jed said, "How can we get wood for our tree house? Will our allowances cover it?"

"I doubt it," said Dad. "But I've got a proposition to make."

"What is it?" asked Bill.

"There's a shed out back that's falling down. If you will take it apart and take out all the old nails, you can have the wood for your tree house."

"You've got yourself a deal," said Jed.

"Sure," said Bill. "We'll start tomorrow."

"Just be careful of the nails," said Dad. "They may be rusty and it could be dangerous if you get scratched."

That night everybody was tired. After a picnic supper Dad lit the fire in the living room. The family was all ready to relax for a while.

"I didn't know moving was such hard work," said Bill.

"There's still lots to do," said Mom. "But the worst of it is over."

"And let's hope we don't ever have to do it again," said Dad. "I like this place and there's plenty of room."

"You know," said Liza, "I think I'm going to like it here after all. My room's really great."

"Hallelujah," said Jed. "That's the first nice thing Liza has said about the house."

"I can't help it if I don't like a haunted house," said Liza. "But I don't think this one really is. It feels just like any other house."

"You wait until John Blake starts walking," said Bill. "You'll believe it then."

"You're just being silly," said Liza. "You don't believe in ghosts either."

"I wouldn't be too sure of that," said Bill. "I have an honest respect for them. Dad, do you think we'll ever see John Blake, or does he just walk when everybody is asleep?"

"You've got me," said Dad. "Never having been acquainted with a ghost, I don't know their habits."

"Stop it, both of you," said Liza.

"Oh, well," said Jed. "If you don't believe in ghosts you won't be able to see them anyway."

"Where did you pick up that bit of wisdom?" asked Dad.

"That's what they say about fairies," said Jed. "So I expect it's true for ghosts, too."

"Who cares?" said Liza. "John Blake can walk all he wants to tonight. I'm so sleepy I'll never know it."

"That's quite enough talk about ghosts," said Mom. "I think it's bedtime for everybody."

5.

A Scare for Liza

Nobody fussed about going to bed that night.
Mom and Dad went upstairs to their room at
the same time the children went to theirs.

Liza undressed and got into bed.

"Gee," she said. "There must be a full moon
tonight. It's so light in here."

She got up and went to the window to see.
Sure enough, the moon was big and round.

"The moonlight makes everything look so ghosty," thought Liza. "I wish Mom and Dad were downstairs with us. But I don't care. I'm going to sleep."

Liza climbed into bed and was asleep minutes later.

A hush settled over the house. Only the chirping of crickets and the croaking of frogs broke the stillness of the night.

Then suddenly a white figure appeared in Liza's doorway. An eerie voice began to chant, "Who is it? Who is there?"

Liza turned in her sleep. The figure standing in the doorway continued to chant, but a little louder.

Liza turned and opened her eyes. Then her scream rang through the night. The white figure glided from the doorway and disappeared. But Liza continued to scream.

Mom and Dad came running. Jed and Bill came soon after.

"What is it? What is it?" they asked.

"Liza, do stop screaming and tell us what happened," said Mom.

Liza began to sob. She said, "The ghost, the ghost was right here, right in my room."

"Oh, come on, baby," said Dad. "You were just having a bad dream."

"No!" shrieked Liza. "It woke me up saying, 'Who is it? Who is there?' "

Jed and Bill were shifting from one foot to the other. They both looked very uncomfortable. Dad saw this.

"All right, boys," he said. "Is this your doing?"

Jed hung his head and said, "Yes."

"But, Dad, we didn't know it would scare her like that," said Bill.

"You knew she was already uneasy about this house. Now look at what you've caused," said Dad.

Both boys looked ashamed.

"We apologize," said Jed. "We really didn't mean to scare you."

"You mean it was you!" sobbed Liza.

"It was Bill with a sheet around him," said Jed. "But I was with him."

"You're mean!" screamed Liza. "You're the most hateful boys I ever saw."

"Shh," said Mom. "That's enough. Just calm down now."

"I think you boys had better go back to your room," said Dad. "But you must be punished for this thoughtlessness. We'll talk about it at breakfast."

The boys went back to their room without a word.

Mom said, "I'll stay with Liza until she gets to sleep."

"In that case," said Dad, "I'll go back to bed. Don't worry, baby. It's all right."

Liza was still clinging to her mother, but she said, "Good night, Dad."

6.
The Mysterious Message

When Liza woke up the next morning, she saw a paper on her window screen.

"Now what could that be?" she asked.

She went over to the window.

"It looks as if a ghost wrote it, sure enough," she said. " 'Welcome to your new home. Follow the clues to a treasure.' Now what does that mean? I better get the boys."

Liza started to go. Then she said, "No, I'm still mad with them. I'll do this myself."

She tried to get the paper, but she could not reach it. It was fastened to the outside of the screen.

"I'll have to go outside for it," said Liza. "But Mom will never let me get out before breakfast. Maybe I will tell the boys after all."

The boys were awake, too.

"Oh, gosh," said Jed. "I forgot. Dad is going to tell us our punishment this morning."

"I wonder what it will be?" asked Bill.

"He'll probably take our allowance away for a while," said Jed.

"I wish we hadn't done that to Liza," said Bill.

"It was your idea," said Jed.

"But you thought it was a good one," said Bill.

"So now we both get punished," said Jed.

Then Liza came in. She said, "I've got the strangest message on my window."

"Your window!" said Bill.

"Yes, on the screen," said Liza. "It looks as if a ghost really wrote it."

"Come on. Let's go and see," said Jed.

But just at that moment Mom called, "Breakfast."

"Now," said Bill, "we'll have to wait."

The children went into the kitchen. Their father was already seated at the table.

"Good morning," he said.

"Good morning, Dad," said the children. Jed and Bill waited to see what he was going to say.

"Your mother and I talked this over, boys," said Dad, "and we think your punishment should be to restrict you to the immediate grounds for the rest of the week. And the grounds do not include the woods. The only exception to that is if Mom or I go with you."

"But, Dad," said Bill, "we'll never get our tree house built before school starts."

"Sorry," said Dad. "That's the way it is."

"Dad," said Jed.

"We'll hear no more about it," said Dad. "That's the punishment."

After they had eaten Dad said, "I must go. I'll meet you people at the restaurant to-night."

"Are we going to eat out?" asked Bill.

"Yes," said Mom. "We'll eat out tonight and tomorrow I'll go grocery shopping."

"Let's go to your room, Liza," said Bill.

The children went into Liza's room. Bill and Jed saw the note on the window.

"Gee," said Bill, "that does look ghosty. But what does the last part say?"

" 'Follow the clues to a treasure,' " said Jed. "Underneath that it says, 'is gate first the garden clue at.' "

"That sure doesn't make sense," said Liza.

"Let me get the paper," said Jed. "Then we can figure it out."

Jed went outside. He was back in just a few minutes, holding the note.

"It's a scrambled sentence," he said.

"Let's unscramble it," said Liza.

"Let's see," said Bill. "I think 'first' and 'clue' go together."

"Yes," said Jed. "And I'll bet 'garden' and 'gate' go together."

"Why couldn't it be, 'garden gate is the first clue'?"

"But that leaves out 'at,' " said Bill.

"Wait a minute," said Jed. "It's 'first clue is at the garden gate.' "

"Let's find the garden gate," said Liza. "Come on."

The children went outside. They ran back of the barn and out to the garden.

"Something *is* there," said Bill. "I can see it already."

Bill untied a paper from the gate. He nodded as he said, "Yep, this is it."

"Is it another scrambled sentence?" asked Liza.

"No," said Bill. "It's worse than that. This time it's scrambled words."

"This is like when we were trying to figure

out the key to the treasure at Grandpa's," said Liza.

"But that time we knew what the treasure was," said Jed. "This time we don't know what we're getting into."

"Here," said Bill, "take a look at this."

Bill held out the paper to Liza and Jed.

They saw: "idfn a cork ttha saw tapinde thiwe."

"Gosh," said Jed. "We'll need pencil and paper for that."

"I'll get some," said Liza.

She ran to the house, and came back quickly with a pencil and paper. She said, "I'll write it down."

Bill said, "Well, at least we know the second word is 'a.' There's no way to scramble that."

"I think the first word is 'find,' " said Jed.

"I'll bet 'saw' is 'was,' " said Liza.

"What do we have now?" asked Bill.

"We've got, 'find a blank blank was blank blank,' " said Liza.

"Could the third word be 'rock'?" asked Jed.

"Sure," said Bill. "And I'll bet the next one is 'that.' "

"Good," said Liza. "Now we have, 'find a rock that was blank blank.' "

"But what could those other words be?" asked Bill.

"Maybe the last one is 'white,' " said Liza.

"That's it," said Jed. " 'Find a rock that was painted white.' "

"Yippee!" said Bill. "We did it!"

"But where are we going to find the rock?" asked Liza.

"Yeah, that's a good question," said Bill. "This place is loaded with rocks."

"But a white one," said Liza. "I've seen

painted rocks in other people's front yards."

"So let's look in our front yard," said Jed.

The children ran to the front yard.

"Look around that flower bed," said Liza. "All those rocks have been painted white."

"Those are bricks, stupid," said Bill. "The clue says a rock."

Then Liza saw something white that was almost hidden by a bush.

"All right," she shouted, "but here's a rock that was painted white. And here's the paper with the third clue on it."

"Let me see, let me see," said Bill. He tried to grab the paper from Liza, but she held on and the paper tore in half.

"Now see what you've done," said Jed. "Give Liza the other piece. She found the clue so she should read it."

"Oh, all right," said Bill. "Here it is."

Liza held the pieces of paper together.

"It's in still another code," she said.

She showed the paper to Bill and Jed. It said:

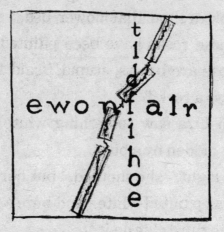

"That really is a hard one," said Bill.

"I think we better tape the pieces together," said Liza. "I have some tape."

"All right," said Jed. "Let's go get it."

In her room, Liza taped the puzzle pieces together.

"Does anybody have any ideas as to where to start with this one?" asked Bill.

All three children were silent. They studied the puzzle for a long time without saying anything.

Then Jed said, "Wait a minute! This might be it. Take the outside letters. See 'tree'?"

"Maybe that is it!" said Bill. "Let's try the next letters."

"The next letters would be 'llow'," said Liza, "and that doesn't make sense."

The children thought some more.

"Maybe we should start in the middle and go around," said Bill. "Let's see, that would be 'faind.' "

"But that's not a word," said Liza.

"No," said Jed. "But 'find' is one and the next word probably is 'a.' "

"What would the next word be?" asked Bill.

"That would be 'hollow,' " said Jed.

"Find a hollow tree," said Bill. "I'll bet that's what the message is."

"And I know where there's a hollow tree," said Liza. "Let's go."

The children ran into the backyard.

"Here it is," said Liza.

"Is there anything in it?" asked Jed.

"Here, I'll see," said Bill. He stood on tiptoe and reached into the tree.

"Success!" he said as he pulled a paper bag out of the tree.

"Do hurry and open it," said Liza.

Bill opened the bag. Inside were three little carved figures and another note.

"Oh, they're darling," said Liza. "May I have the rabbit?"

"Sure," said Bill. "I like the owl."

"I'm glad you said that," said Jed, "because I like the fox."

"What does the note say?" asked Liza. "Is it in another code?"

"I forgot about the note," said Bill. "No, it's not in code, but it's in that ghosty writing. It says, 'go to the hollow tree again tomorrow.' "

"Gee," said Jed, "this is fun. But who is doing it?"

"Maybe it is the ghost," said Bill.

"The handwriting sure looks spooky enough," said Liza. "Can a ghost write?"

"You've got me," said Jed. "I wish I knew more about ghosts."

"Whoever this is carves very well," said Liza.

"I wonder if John Blake knew how to carve?" asked Bill.

"We can find out about that," said Liza. "There's Mr. Hobbs."

"Mr. Hobbs!" said Bill. "What's he doing here?"

"Mom said he was going to work in the yard for a few days," said Liza.

"Let's ask him," said Jed.

The children ran to Mr. Hobbs.

"Mr. Hobbs," said Liza. "You knew John Blake, didn't you?"

"Sure did," said Mr. Hobbs. "He was a great friend of mine."

"Did he know how to carve?" asked Bill.

"Now what made you ask that question?" asked Mr. Hobbs. "What are you children up to?"

"Oh, nothing," said Bill. "We just wanted to know."

48

"As a matter of fact," said Mr. Hobbs, "John Blake did carve. He was quite clever in making animals out of chips of wood."

"He was!" said the children. They looked at one another.

"Now what is this about?" asked Mr. Hobbs.

"It's just a game we're playing," said Jed. "Come on, let's get back to it."

"Thank you, Mr. Hobbs," said Liza.

7.
The Old Shed

"Now, how about that?" said Bill. "Maybe I do believe in ghosts after all."

"I wonder what a ghost looks like," said Jed.

"I always think of them as being white and shapeless and floating around," said Liza.

"I think they look like the person whose ghost they are," said Bill, "but that you can sort of see through them."

"Yeah," said Jed, "I think of them like that, too."

"I wish we could go to the woods," said Bill.

"Let's get busy and take down that old shed," said Jed. "At least we'll be getting something done about the tree house."

"Okay," said Bill. "Race you to the tool shed."

The boys raced, but Liza followed more slowly.

"How are we going to work this?" asked Bill. "There are only two hammers."

"We'll use the hammers to knock the shed apart," said Jed. "And, Liza, you can use a rock to get the nails out."

"All right," said Liza. "I'll find one now."

The boys began hammering at the shed.

"Dad's right," said Jed. "This wood is still good. I was afraid it would be rotten."

"He's right about the nails being rusty,

too," said Bill. "Here, Liza, here's the first board for you."

Liza took a stone and pounded at the nails. The stone slipped and her arm came down on a nail.

"Oh, gosh," said Liza. "I've scratched my arm on a rusty nail."

The boys looked at the bleeding arm.

"Better go and tell Mom," said Jed.

Liza ran to the house calling, "Mom! Mom! Come quickly!"

Mom met Liza at the door.

"Oh, dear," she said. "What did you do to your arm?"

"Scratched it on a rusty nail," said Liza.

"A rusty nail!" said Mom. "Well, let's clean it up. Then I'm going to call Dr. Hunt to see if you should get a tetanus shot."

"I hope not," said Liza.

But when Mom called Dr. Hunt, he said that by all means Liza should have a shot.

Mom hung up the telephone and said, "Liza, call the boys in. We need them, too."

The boys came when Liza called.

"What is it?" asked Bill. "Don't you know we're working?"

"Mom wants you," said Liza.

"Yes, boys," said Mom. "I just talked with Dr. Hunt. He thinks Liza should have a tetanus shot and that each of you boys should have one just as a precaution."

"Gosh, Mom," said Jed. "Isn't that taking it a little far? Liza gets scratched and we have to take shots."

"Sorry," said Mom, "but I'm not taking any chances. You're all working on those old boards, and there are lots of rusty nails in them. Now wash your faces and let's go."

The children went glumly to their rooms.

A little later they were all in the car on their way to see Dr. Hunt.

"If I had a hammer," said Liza, "this wouldn't have happened."

"Don't you have a hammer?" asked Mom. "I thought we had several of them."

"Only two," said Bill. "We sure could use a third one."

"I think you're right," said Mom. "If you're going to make a tree house, you'll need three. After we see Dr. Hunt we'll go by the hardware store and get another one. How's that?"

"Great," said Liza. "It wasn't easy to bang out those nails with a rock."

"Nor was it safe," said Mom.

The children soon had their shots and were ready to go.

"That wasn't too bad," said Bill. "At least we got lollipops out of it."

"Let's go by the hardware store now," said Mom. "Suppose you boys go in and get the hammer. You know the kind you need."

When the boys came back with the hammer, they handed it to Liza.

"Since you're the one who got hurt, you can have the new hammer first," said Bill.

"Thanks a lot," said Liza.

"But I don't think you'll get to use it for a while," said Mom. "That cloud looks as if it could start pouring any minute now."

Mom was right. They had just gotten into the house when the rain started.

8.

The Attic

"Okay," said Bill. "What shall we do now?"

"I know!" said Liza. "The attic! Mom said the attic was a rainy-day job and this sure is a rainy day."

"Hey, that's right," said Bill. "I had forgotten all about the attic. Okay, Mom?"

"Sure," said Mom. "I'll call you when it's time to dress and go meet Dad."

The children scrambled up the stairs to the attic. Liza turned on the light.

"Boy, I'll say this is a mess," she said. "Look at those stacks of old magazines."

"Magazines and that old clock seem to be about all there is," said Jed. "I have a feeling this is going to be boring."

"But look," said Bill. "Over there underneath a pile of magazines. There's a trunk. Old trunks usually have something interesting in them."

"Well, it looks hopeful anyway," said Jed. "Let's get it cleared off so we can open it."

It didn't take the children long to throw the magazines off the trunk. When Bill opened it, bugs scurried everywhere.

"Ugh!" said Liza. "I don't want any part of that."

"Sissy," said Bill. "Those bugs won't hurt you."

He began throwing things out of the trunk.

"There seems to be nothing but old clothes in it," said Jed.

"Hey now, hold on," said Bill.

A few minutes later Bill shouted, "See, I told you so."

He pulled out a helmet and a brown case.

"Jeepers!" said Jed. "You really did find something. Let's see what's in the case."

Bill opened the case and took out a weird-looking mask with a long tube at the front. He put the mask on.

"Oh, take it off, Bill," said Liza. "It's too scary."

Bill took off the mask and said, "Here, Jed, you try it on and let me see."

Jed put the mask on and Liza turned the other way.

"Boy," said Bill, "that *is* scary! Here, let me put on the mask and the helmet."

"Please don't," said Liza, "or I'm going to leave."

"Oh, come on, Liza," said Jed. "Be a sport."

"Do you suppose these belonged to John Blake?" asked Bill.

"Could be," said Jed. "We'll ask Dad about them."

"Let's hang them in our room," said Bill.

"That's a good idea," said Jed. "I think they came from the First World War."

"What do you suppose the mask was used for?" asked Bill.

"It's a gas mask," said Jed.

"Well, it sure could have been used to scare people," said Liza.

"Let's see what else we can find," said Bill. "Take a look at the dates on these magazines. Do you think they're valuable?"

"No," said Jed. "Can't you see they're falling apart and bugs are eating them?"

"All right, all right," said Bill. "Golly, this must be a picture of the very first airplane."

"Of course it is, stupid," said Jed. "Don't you see it says 'Kitty Hawk' right here?"

"I didn't notice," said Bill, and gave Jed a push.

"And stop pushing me," said Jed. He gave Bill a hard push backward so that Bill hit the clock.

"So you want to fight, do you?" said Bill.

"Look!" said Liza. She pointed to the clock. The boys stopped fighting and looked.

"Look at what?" asked Bill. "I don't see anything."

"Down here," said Liza. "When you hit the clock, Bill, this started to open."

Both boys dropped down beside Liza.

"Gee," said Jed. "Maybe it's a secret hiding place. Let me see if I can open it farther."

Jed tried to pull the panel back, but it wouldn't move.

"No, I'm afraid I'll break it if I pull too hard," he said. "Bill, where did you hit it? There must be a secret button somewhere."

"Are you nuts?" said Bill. "How do I know where I hit it!"

"We'll just have to search the whole thing," said Liza. She began pressing here and there.

"Children," called Mom. "Come on down and get washed and dressed."

"Oh, no!" said all three children.

"Can't we stay just a little longer?" asked Bill.

"Sorry," said Mom. "We'll have to hurry to make it now."

"Wouldn't you know it?" said Jed.

"Okay," said Bill. "But secret's the word and you remember that, Liza."

"Don't worry," said Liza. "I know how to keep a secret."

The children started downstairs.

"Oh, the helmet and mask," said Jed. "Here, I'll get them."

"Did you have fun?" asked Mom.

"Yes," said Bill. "And we have something to show you."

"Can it wait until we get back?" asked Mom. "Your father doesn't like to be kept waiting."

"All right," said Bill. "It will keep."

"That place is a mess," said Liza.

"And the three of you are messes, too," said Mom. "Do hurry and get ready."

"We'll be right with you," said Bill, as the children went to their rooms.

9.
Delayed Plans

Dad was waiting for them at the restaurant.

After they had ordered Bill said, "Dad, we found John Blake's helmet and gas mask."

"You did!" said Dad. "How do you know they were his?"

"Well, we don't really," said Bill. "But why else would they be in his attic?"

"That's as good a reason as any," said Dad.

"But the gas mask scares me," said Liza,

"with that long tube coming down from it."

Dad laughed. "I know what you mean, Liza. My older brother used to put my father's mask on to scare me."

"He did!" said Liza. "I can't imagine Uncle Matt doing that."

"Oh, he did a lot of things to keep me in line," said Dad.

"Dad, may we hang the helmet and mask in our room?" asked Bill.

"I don't see why not," said Dad. "But you had better check with Mom. That's her department."

"Sure, hang them up," said Mom. "Everything else gets hung on your walls."

"There are stacks of old, old magazines up there, too," said Jed.

"Yes," said Liza, "and everything is full of bugs. Bill opened an old trunk and bugs ran all over the place."

"Bugs!" said Mom. "Remind me to spray

tomorrow. I'll not have them getting into other parts of the house. Bugs! Ugh!"

"There's a big old clock up there, too," said Jed. "It's taller than I am."

"It may be a grandfather clock," said Dad.

"I think it is," said Liza.

"I've always wanted a grandfather clock," said Dad. "We'll see if we can get it in working order."

"And, Dad," said Liza, "it has—"

Bill kicked Liza just at that moment.

"Yes," said Dad. "It has what?"

"Oh, it has carvings. Yes, that's it," said Liza. "It has carvings all over it."

"I'll take a look at it," said Dad. "And now here's our food."

"Oh, boy," said Bill. "I'm sure ready for it."

Everybody was hungry so there was very little conversation while they ate.

On the way home, Jed said, "Mom, can we go back up to the attic?"

"Indeed not," said Mom. "It's just too dirty and you've all had baths."

"But, Mom," said Bill.

"No," said Mom. "There's nothing up there that won't keep until tomorrow."

The children were quiet the rest of the way home. Mom had used that 'don't argue with me' tone and they knew she wouldn't give in.

When they went into the house Bill said, "Let's go to our room. Do you want to come, Liza?"

"I guess so," said Liza. "There's nothing else to do. Jed, why did you have to ask if we could go to the attic? Maybe Mom wouldn't have said anything if we had just gone."

"I'm sorry," said Jed. "It never occurred to me that she wouldn't let us."

"Now we have to wait until tomorrow," said Liza. "And by that time Mom will have a dozen other things for us to do."

"Can't help it," said Jed. "That's the way it is."

"One thing, we've got to keep Dad from going up and looking at that old clock. He might see the crack."

"He won't go tonight," said Liza. "And you know Dad. He'll have forgotten about it tomorrow if we don't mention it."

"So remember, secret's the word where the old clock is concerned."

"Agreed," said Bill.

"Agreed," said Liza.

10.
Three Kittens

Liza went to her room. She looked out of the window.

"The hollow tree!" she said. "I can see it from my window. That gives me an idea."

Liza went back into the boys' room.

"Say," she said, "I can see the hollow tree from my window."

"You can!" said Bill. "Why don't we stay

up tonight and try to find out who is leaving the messages?"

"I've got a better idea," said Jed. "Why don't we stay up in shifts? One of us can watch until he gets sleepy and then he can wake the next person up."

"That's a neat idea," said Bill. "All right with you, Liza?"

"Sure," said Liza. "I'll take the first shift."

At bedtime the children went into Liza's room to make the final plans.

"I'll put this big chair by the window," said Liza. "Then I can sit in it and see the tree, too."

"Now remember, Liza, as soon as you get sleepy," said Bill, "you call me. Is that all right, Jed?"

"Yes," said Jed. "Then I'll take a turn after you and call Liza."

Soon the house was all in darkness. Liza sat by the window with her eyes glued to the tree. It wasn't long before she began to feel sleepy. She stood up awhile to see if that would help. Then she sat down again.

Liza thought, "I'm going to sleep. I've got to get Bill up."

She went to the boys' room. Bill and Jed were both sleeping. Liza went to Bill's bed and called, "Bill, Bill, wake up. It's your turn."

Bill just turned over. Finally Liza shook him.

"Huh?" said Bill. "What is it? What is it?"

"It's your turn to watch," said Liza.

Bill sat up and rubbed his eyes.

"Oh, all right," he said.

They went back into Liza's room. Bill went to the chair and Liza went to bed. In a very few minutes she was asleep.

Bill sat in the chair. He was trying his best to stay awake, but his eyes were growing heavier and heavier.

Suddenly Bill opened his eyes and sat up straight. It was morning and the sun was streaming in the window.

"I went to sleep after all," said Bill. "What will Liza and Jed say?"

Jed came into Liza's room just as she was waking up.

"Bill, what happened?" said Jed. "Why didn't you call me?"

"I—I went to sleep," said Bill.

"For gosh sakes," said Jed. "Well, come on and let's get dressed so we can see if there is a message in the hollow tree."

"Wait for me," said Liza.

"Okay," said Jed, "but hurry up."

In a few minutes the children were ready to go. But as they passed the kitchen Mom called, "Don't go out until you've had your breakfast."

"Gee, Mom," said Bill. "Not even for a minute?"

"Nope," said Mom. "Breakfast is on the table."

While they were eating Mom said, "Now today I want you to clean out all the old magazines and rags in the attic. They only pick up rubbish once a week out here and tomorrow's the day."

"Do we have to do it right now?" asked Bill.

"No," said Mom. "Any time today will be all right."

"May we be excused now?" asked Liza.

"Certainly," said Mom. "I'll remind you about the attic later on."

The children went outdoors and ran to the tree. Bill was the first to get there. He reached into the hollow and pulled out a piece of paper. Jed and Liza waited impatiently for him to unfold and read it.

"What does it say?" asked Jed.

"Your guess is as good as mine," said Bill. "It's in another code."

"Another one!" said Jed. "Our ghost sure knows a lot about codes."

"I still wonder who is doing this," said Liza.

"Do you suppose it could be Mr. Hobbs?" asked Bill.

"No," said Jed. "He was too surprised when we asked him about the carved animals."

"Maybe he was just acting," said Bill.

"Well, whoever it is," said Jed, "let's get on with it and see what we are supposed to do next. Let's see the message, Bill."

Bill handed the paper to Jed. Liza came over to see it, too. It said:

"skcitshcribehtwollof."

"This is the hardest one yet," said Liza.

"And we don't have a clue as to what to do with it," said Bill.

"This is going to take work," said Jed. "Let's get started."

"I brought a pencil and pad with me," said Liza.

The children sat on some rocks and tried to figure out what to do with the letters.

"I see some words in it," said Liza. "There's 'it,' 'crib,' 'two,' 'of.'"

"That doesn't make sense," said Bill. "Try something else."

The children sat for a long time just think-ing. Finally Jed said, "Maybe this is back-ward writing."

"Try it and see," said Bill.

Jed took the pencil and pad and began to write. Then he showed Liza and Bill the results:

"followthebirchsticks."

"That's it," said Liza. "I see it now. It says, 'follow the birch sticks.'"

"But what does that mean?" asked Bill.

"Just what it says," said Jed. "I see a birch stick right under your foot."

"I see another one over there," said Bill. "Come on, let's follow them."

The sticks were spread far apart and sometimes the children had to really look to find them.

The sticks led them around the barn and toward a field that was back of the house.

"Gosh," said Jed. "I hope they don't go into the woods."

But a few minutes later Liza spotted a box by the big rock pile.

"I bet that's it!" she said.

"Let's go see," said Bill.

The children ran toward the box. Before they got there they could hear a mewing sound.

"Cats," said Jed. "I'll bet it's cats."

And sure enough when they lifted the box they found three little kittens in it.

"Oh, they're adorable!" said Liza. "Look at that little black one. May I have him?"

"Sure," said Jed. "I want the gray one."

"That leaves the striped one for me," said Bill. "It really doesn't matter. They're all so cute."

"That reminds me," said Liza. "Mary and Jimmy said their uncle had kittens and they would get one for us."

"We sure don't need another one now," said Jed.

"I miss Mary and Jimmy," said Bill.

"I wish they lived closer," said Jed. "There are no children out here."

"Maybe Mom will let us invite them out next week," said Bill.

"They're visiting their Uncle Dan sometime during the vacation," said Liza.

"We better get back to the house," said Jed. "What will Mom say when we come home with three cats?"

"She'll probably blow her stack," said Bill.

"At least she can't make us return them because we don't know where they came from."

They met Mr. Hobbs on the way back to the house.

"Well, now look at those kittens," he said. "Where did you get them?"

"We found them in the field," said Bill.

"It will seem natural to have cats around again," said Mr. Hobbs.

"What do you mean?" asked Jed.

"John Blake always had a bunch of cats," said Mr. Hobbs.

"He did!" said the children.

"Yes," said Mr. Hobbs. "He didn't care for dogs, but I've seen as many as six or eight cats here at one time."

"Three is enough for us," said Bill.

The children went on toward the house.

"Gosh," said Liza. "You know, I really believe John Blake's ghost *is* doing all of this."

"At least he's a friendly ghost," said Bill.

When they got near the house, they called to Mom. She was in the kitchen. The children took the kittens inside.

"Three kittens!" said Mom. "One I can see, but do we need three?"

"Oh, Mom," said Liza. "Cats aren't much trouble."

"Yeah, Mom," said Bill. "We'll take care of them."

"Where did you get them?" asked Mom.

"We found them in our field in a box," said Jed.

"In that case," said Mom, "I guess you'll have to keep them."

"Can we feed them?" asked Liza.

"Sure," said Mom. "I'll get you a pan of milk."

Mom got a pan and poured milk into it.

"Do put it on a piece of newspaper," said Mom. "I don't want milk all over the floor."

Bill got the newspaper and Liza set the pan of milk on top of it. They put the kittens around it. The kittens were funny. First they put their paws into the milk. Then they got their noses in it and that made them sneeze. Soon Mom was laughing as hard as the children at the kittens.

"They're real little clowns," said Mom.

"Where can we keep them?" asked Liza.

"On the back porch until they get a little bigger," said Mom. "I'll get an old baking pan and you can put some dirt in it for a litter pan."

"All right," said Liza. "I'll do that now."

The children took the kittens to the back porch and played with them for a long time.

11.
Spoiled Plans

Mom called the children in. She said, "I think you had better start on the attic now."

"All right, Mom," said Bill. "But that's a lot of work to do in one day."

"I'll help you," said Mom.

The children looked at one another.

"You don't have to help, Mom," said Jed. "We can do it."

"But I don't mind," said Mom. "Bill is right. It is a lot of work."

"You said the attic could be our project, Mom," said Liza. "We want to do it all."

"All right," said Mom. "But it must be done today. Yell if you need help."

The children went to the attic.

"Why did Mom have to decide this all of a sudden?" asked Liza.

"It's all your fault," said Bill.

"My fault!" said Liza.

"Yes, you and your bugs," said Bill. "You know how Mom feels about bugs and you had to tell her last night."

"Now come on, Bill," said Jed. "Mom's never acted that way before. How could Liza know?"

"She should have known," said Bill. "You know Mom starts screaming every time she sees anything that crawls."

"Okay, okay," said Liza. "It was all my

fault. I'm sorry. Now let's get started or Mom will be up here for sure."

"Yes," said Jed. "And it will take all morning to get this done."

"Each time we pass that old clock the crack will be there," said Bill. "And we can't find out what's in it."

"If we work as fast as we can," said Jed, "maybe Mom won't make us do anything this afternoon. Then we'll have lots of time to get the clock open."

"I wouldn't bet on it," said Bill.

"Come on, let's get going," said Liza.

All morning the children carted load after load of junk from the attic to the backyard. Mom kept offering to help, but the children insisted they could do it all.

Finally they finished. The last magazine and box of rags had been taken out.

But the big blow was yet to come. At lunch Mom said, "Now I'm going to spray the whole attic with insecticide and close the door. By tomorrow the bugs should be dead."

"Mom," said Liza, "can't we play up there?"

"Not today," said Mom. "Besides the sun is shining and you should get outside. You might take the kittens with you."

"Want me to spray for you, Mom?" asked Jed.

"No," said Mom. "I don't want you around insecticide. I'll have to do this job."

"Please, Mom, let us do it," said Bill.

"You're being very sweet, but I'd rather do this myself," said Mom.

She went and got the can of insecticide and went to the attic.

"Do you think she'll notice the clock?" asked Liza.

"I doubt it," said Jed. "Mom has murder, bug murder, in her eyes today."

"I'll feel better when she gets through," said Bill.

"We might as well go outside," said Jed. "That sure spoils our plans for today."

The children took the kittens out in the yard and played with them for a while.

"I'm going to name my kitten Blackie," said Liza.

"I'll call mine Butterball," said Jed. "He's so fat."

"I guess I'll call mine Tiger," said Bill.

"He's the same color as a tiger and has stripes."

A little later the children carried the kittens back to the porch.

"What do you think is in the clock?" asked Liza.

"It may be a treasure map," said Jed.

"Do you really think so?" asked Bill. "Then you think maybe John Blake left a hidden treasure?"

"You've got me," said Jed.

"Oh, why did I have to mention bugs?" said Liza. "Maybe Mom wouldn't have thought of any of this."

"Too late to do anything about it now," said Jed.

Mom came back downstairs.

"Now," she said, "that's done."

Jed said, "Let's go back to that shed. I'd like to finish it today."

"Right with you," said Bill.

"Just let me get the new hammer," said Liza.

The children went out to the shed. They worked for a while in silence. Then Jed said, "Do you suppose Dad is doing these puzzles?"

"Dad!" said Bill and Liza.

"He's never done anything like this before," said Bill. "What makes you think it's Dad?"

"I don't know," said Jed. "It was just an idea."

"Maybe we can find out," said Bill.

"How?" asked Liza.

"We can set a trap to get his footprint," said Bill. "Then we can take one of his shoes and compare it with the print."

"But suppose it is the ghost," said Liza. "Do you think a ghost would make a footprint?"

"I don't know," said Bill.

"I don't think it would," said Jed. "I think ghosts sort of float around."

"What kind of trap can we set?" asked Liza.

"Maybe we could put flour all around the tree," said Bill.

"No," said Jed. "That's no good. He might see that. There must be another way."

"I know!" said Liza. "We can put loose dirt around the tree. He wouldn't notice that and we could get a print."

"That's a good idea," said Jed. "Then if we don't get a print, we'll know it's the ghost."

"Come on, let's do it now," said Bill.

"No," said Jed. "It would be better to do it late this afternoon. Somebody might notice if we do it now."

"Besides, we have this shed to finish," said Liza.

12.
The Trap

After supper the children went outside. Dad was there.

"Look at Dad," whispered Bill. "See how he's looking at that hollow tree?"

"Maybe he is our ghost after all," whispered Liza.

"Hi, Dad," called Jed. "What's up?"

"Just looking at this hollow tree," said

Dad. "It's such a nice tree I would hate to have it die. I think I'd better get a tree surgeon out to fill up that hole."

"Oh, no!" said the children.

"Why not?" asked Dad.

"Because—because—" started Bill.

"Because we like hollow trees," said Liza.

"That's right," said Bill. "We like hollow trees."

"But Dad's right," said Jed. "It would be a pity for the tree to die."

"Well, don't worry," said Dad. "I think things like that are done in the fall anyway. So you can have your hollow tree until then."

Dad went into the house.

"Gee, that was close," said Bill. "Do you still think it's Dad?"

"It could be," said Jed. "Maybe he was trying to fool us with the talk about the tree dying."

"Anyway," said Liza, "we'll find out tonight when we get his footprint."

"We better get that loose dirt now," said Jed. "It will soon be dark."

"Where shall we get it?" asked Liza.

"Better go by the old shed," said Jed. "A hole there won't be noticed."

The children went out to the shed.

"We're dopes," said Bill. "We didn't bring anything to put the dirt in."

"I'll get a shovel and a bucket," said Jed. He went and got the tools.

"Bill and I will do the digging and the carrying," he said. "Liza, you spread it around."

"Okay," said Liza. "I'll wait for you by the tree."

Jed and Bill carried several buckets of dirt to the tree. Liza carefully spread it in a big circle.

"There," she said. "That should do it."

Later that night Dad said, "Gee, I'm in the mood for some rummy. Any takers?"

"I'll play with you," said Jed.

"So will I," said Bill.

"How about you, Liza?" said Dad. "Want to play?"

"I don't think so," said Liza.

"In that case," said Mom, "I need Liza. I want her to try on some dresses so I can get the hems done. Okay, Liza?"

"Sure, Mom," said Liza.

The boys and Dad went into the living room to play cards.

Liza went with Mom into her bedroom to try on dresses.

"Gee, Mom," said Liza, "when do you think we can have that party?"

"Oh, just about any time after school starts again," said Mom. "We won't start any of the painting until summer. The only other thing I would really like to get done is the basement. I think it would be fun to have the party there. There's so much room."

"That would be neat," said Liza. "But what has to be done in the basement? It looks fine to me."

"Just a good cleaning and some furniture for it. You know, a few chairs and a table or two," said Mom.

"We can help with the cleaning," said Liza.

"If we can get it done before school starts, I see no reason why you can't have your party whenever you want it," said Mom.

"Mom," said Liza, "can we invite Miss Matthewson? She said she wanted to see the house."

"Certainly," said Mom, "and we'll invite Jed's teacher, too. What kind of party are you planning to have?"

"Since this is supposed to be a haunted house," said Liza, "could we have something spooky?"

"I don't see why not," said Mom. "But you children will have to make the plans. I'm not very good at that, though I'll help you as much as I can."

"Oh, Mom! You're great!" said Liza. She threw her arms around her mother and hugged her.

"Hey, hold it," said Mom. "You won't think I'm so great if you get stuck with pins. But this is the last dress."

"Good," said Liza. "I want to tell the boys about the party. Then we can start making plans for it right away. I want it to be the best party we've ever had."

"Okay," said Mom. "Off with you and let me get my work done."

Liza ran to the living room and told the boys.

"That's a great idea," said Jed. "Maybe we could make ghosts out of paper or sheets and put them in unexpected places."

"Oh, we need Mary and Jimmy," said Bill. "They're great at making things."

"Yes!" said Liza. "We'll have to get them to help."

"Do you think we could invite them out?" asked Jed.

"Sure," said Dad. "Maybe they could come for an overnight visit."

"Good," said Bill. "Dad, do you think we could have some weird noises for the party? How could we do that?"

"You could use the tape recorder," said Dad. "I expect you children could make as weird noises as anybody and we'll record them."

"We'll really have some party!" said Bill.

The children went on discussing other ideas for the party. The ideas got wilder and wilder. Finally Dad said, "Wait a minute! If you get your party too scary, everybody will turn around and go home."

"And speaking of going," said Mom, "it's time, past time, for three children I know to go to bed."

"Gee, Mom," said Bill. "Just when we were getting started on our plans."

"There's always tomorrow," said Mom. "Now go along with you."

"Okay, okay," said Bill.

The children said their good-nights and went to their rooms.

13.
Footprints

The next morning the children were up early. Right after breakfast they started to go out. But Mom called them.

"Just a minute," she said. "What about the kittens? They would like some breakfast, too. I bought some cat food for them."

"I'll feed them," said Liza. Bill and Jed played with the kittens while Liza fixed the food.

"There you are," said Liza. She put the food down. The kittens tumbled over one another in their hurry to get to the bowl.

"They really are cute," said Bill. "But come on, we've got other things to do."

The children ran to the hollow tree.

"Hey, look," said Jed. "There are footprints."

"Here's a good one," said Liza. "We can compare it with one of Dad's shoes."

"At least we know now that it wasn't a ghost," said Jed.

"But look at this mishmash of other footprints!" said Bill. "They're small. They look like children's prints."

"They do at that," said Jed. "But we don't know any children out here."

"Say, Liza," said Bill. "Are you sure it's not Dad and you who are doing this?"

"Me!" said Liza. "Why not you or Jed? Why me?"

"Sorry," said Bill. "It was just a thought."

"Come on," said Jed. "Let's look in the hollow tree."

"But do be careful," said Liza, "and don't mess up the footprints."

"All right, all right," said Bill. He reached into the hollow tree and pulled out a piece of paper.

"Is it in code today?" asked Liza.

"It sure is," said Bill.

"Let us see it, too," said Jed.

Bill handed him the paper. It said:

"igbayursayrisepayotayorrowmay."

"Gosh," said Liza. "That doesn't make any sense at all."

"We'll need a pencil and paper to solve this," said Jed.

"And a few good ideas, too," said Bill.

"Let's go to my room," said Liza.

The children went inside and to Liza's room. She got a pencil and paper.

"Is it written backward again?" asked Bill.

"I don't know," said Jed. "We'll try it and see."

Jed copied the letters backward. When he got through he showed the others what it looked like:

"yamworroyatoyapesiryasruyabgi."

"That doesn't help one bit," said Liza.

"Does anybody else have an idea?" asked Jed.

"Not a one," said Bill. "Maybe it doesn't say anything."

"I think it does," said Jed, "if we can just figure it out."

The children studied the puzzle for a long time. Finally Liza said, "I think I get it!"

"You do?" said Jed and Bill.

"Let me hold it a minute," said Liza.

"Hurry up and tell us your idea," said Bill.

"Well, you see the 'ays'?" said Liza.

"Yes," said Jed. "What about them?"

"I think they separate the words," said Liza.

"Show me," said Bill.

Liza took the paper and began to write. When she got through it looked like this:

"igb urs risep ot orrowm."

"Well, that doesn't make any sense," said Bill.

"Oh, sure!" said Jed. "It's Pig Latin!"

"Pig Latin!" said Bill.

"Of course," said Jed. "Having it all run together is what made it so hard."

"Yes," said Liza, "Mary and I used to write notes to each other in Pig Latin."

"I still don't get it," said Bill.

"You will," said Jed. "It's simple now that the 'ays' are out of the way. Now we just take the last letter and put it first."

"So do it," said Bill.

Jed copied the words on paper.

"See," he said. "It says, 'big surprise tomorrow.' "

"Okay. But what does that mean?" asked Bill.

"I have a feeling we'll have to wait until tomorrow to find out," said Jed.

"The footprints!" said Bill. "I forgot all about them."

"I did, too," said Jed.

"Come on, let's get one of Dad's shoes and try it out," said Bill.

"You go get the shoe," said Liza. "Mom might get suspicious if all three of us go upstairs."

"We'll meet you outside," said Jed.

In a few minutes Bill joined the other two at the tree.

"How shall we do this?" he asked.

"Let's put it next to the footprint and see if it matches," said Liza.

"Oh, for gosh sakes!" said Bill. "I brought
a left shoe and that's a right shoe print."

"Here," said Liza. "I'll go change the
shoe."

Liza was back very quickly.

"Now," said Bill, "put it right next to that
print."

"Well," said Jed after a moment, "they're

not really the same, but they're awfully close."

"Maybe Dad had on a different pair of shoes when he walked here," said Liza. "Wouldn't that make a difference?"

"I guess it would," said Bill.

"Oh, phooey," said Jed. "After all that, we really don't know any more than we did before. It could be Dad or it could be someone else."

"It's those small footprints that worry me," said Bill. "I still think they belong to children."

"You've got me," said Jed. "But I'll bet we find out tomorrow."

14.
The Old Clock

"Hey," said Bill, "what about the old clock?
We can go to the attic today."

"Yippee!" said Jed. "Let's go."

When they went inside Mom was dressed
to go out.

"Where are you going?" asked Liza.

"I've got some shopping to do," said Mom.
"If I don't get back in time you children fix

your own lunch. There are plenty of sandwich makings here."

"Don't worry, Mom," said Jed. "We won't go hungry."

"All right," said Mom. "The house is yours for the morning."

Mom went out. As soon as Bill heard the car start, he shouted, "Hurray! Freedom at last. Now we can see what's in that clock."

"Let's go," said Jed.

The children raced up the steps to the attic. Liza opened the door. She said, "Gosh, it stinks. Do open that window."

Jed tried to open the window, but it wouldn't budge.

"Hey, Bill," he said, "I need help. We've got to have some air in this place."

With the two boys working together the window finally opened.

"Now," said Bill, "to work."

"I was thinking about this," said Jed. "And I have a feeling the button or whatever it is is in one of the carvings. Let's concentrate on those."

"Okay," said Liza.

The children carefully punched each carving.

"Gosh, this could take all day," said Bill. "There are so many carvings."

"Just be sure not to miss any," said Liza. "That would be just the one we want."

A little later Bill shouted, "Hey, I found it! At least this one moves."

Liza and Jed looked.

"It closed it," said Bill. "Pooh. Here I've closed it before we even opened it."

"Bill, which one moved?" asked Jed.

"This one," said Bill. He pointed to the center of a carved flower just below the door.

"Then let's press all the ones along the top and bottom," said Jed.

Jed began to punch the center of the carved flowers above the door. Finally he found one that moved. Slowly the door began to open.

"But I pushed all of those before and nothing happened," said Liza.

"You must have missed that one," said Jed.

"Yeah," said Bill. "And you were the one who was telling us to be careful."

"Oh, it doesn't matter," said Jed. "Let's see if there's anything in there."

Jed reached in, but he came out empty-handed.

"Nothing," he said.

"Oh, phooey!" said Bill. "After all that, nothing."

Bill kicked the clock. A roll of paper fell from behind it.

"Hey, what's that?" asked Jed. He picked up the roll of paper.

"Gee, maybe it's a treasure map after all," said Bill. "Hurry up and unroll it, Jed."

Jed unrolled the paper.

"But what is it?" asked Liza. "It doesn't make any sense to me."

"It looks like house plans," said Bill.

"We'll soon find out," said Jed. "But let's go downstairs. This place still stinks."

"Okay," said Bill.

"Let's close the secret door first," said Jed. "We may want to use it ourselves."

"Oh, let me close it," said Liza.

"Be my guest," said Jed.

Liza quickly closed the secret door and hurried after the boys.

15.
House Plans

"Get me some books to hold this flat," said Jed.

Liza brought the books. Jed unrolled the plans and weighted them down at each corner.

"Hey," said Bill. "I think these are the plans for this house. See, that's the living room and there's the dining room. And over here is our room."

"I think you're right," said Jed. "But why were the plans hidden behind the clock and not in it?"

"Maybe the roll was too long to fit in the clock," said Liza.

"Or, maybe they weren't hidden at all," said Jed. "Maybe they just happened to be there."

"I don't think so," said Bill. "With all that space, why should they be behind the clock? I think they were hidden."

"But why hide house plans?" asked Jed. "There's nothing valuable about them."

"I think there must have been some reason for keeping them a secret," said Bill.

"I don't know what it could be," said Jed.

The children studied the plans carefully.

"Wait a minute," said Bill. "Is the basement really like that?"

"What do you mean?" asked Jed. "What's different about it?"

"This," said Bill, pointing. "I don't remember a room under Liza's room."

"You're right," said Jed. "I hadn't noticed that."

"Do you remember seeing a room there, Liza?" asked Bill.

"Nope," said Liza.

"Let's go," said Jed. "We can find the answer to that right away."

The children ran down the basement stairs.

"You see," said Bill. "There's nothing but a blank wall there."

"That's funny," said Liza.

"Maybe those aren't the plans to this house after all," said Bill.

"I think they are," said Jed. "Everything else is where it belongs."

"Do you think they put up the wall after

they built the house?" asked Liza.

"They may have," said Jed. "But why wall up a room?"

"Maybe it's a secret room!" said Bill.

"Come off it, Bill," said Jed. "You only find secret rooms in storybooks."

"I don't believe that," said Bill. "Somebody must have had a real secret room or how would anybody know to write about them?"

"Maybe Bill's right," said Liza. "Maybe it is a secret room. Maybe they had something to hide."

"Do you think there could be a treasure hidden there?" asked Jed.

"It could be," said Bill. "Or they might have used it to torture people in."

"Maybe it was a secret hideaway for gangsters," said Jed.

"Maybe they killed somebody and had to hide the body," said Bill.

116

"Stop it!" said Liza. "That gives me the shivers, to think of sleeping over a dead body."

"Can you think of a better reason for needing a secret room?" asked Jed.

"I can't think of any reason," said Liza.

"Maybe there's a door outside," said Bill.

"Let's look and see," said Liza.

The children went outside, but again they were faced with a solid brick wall.

"I think we should look in Liza's room," said Jed. "There might be a clue there."

"Good idea," said Bill.

The children went inside and to Liza's room.

"But what do we look for?" asked Liza.

"They had to have some way to get in," said Jed. "Maybe there's a secret door."

"A door to that room would have to be in the floor," said Bill.

"Let's divide the room into three parts so each of us can study a part of the floor," said Jed.

"All right," said Liza. "Bill, you take from here to here. Jed, you take from here to the corner, and I'll take the rest."

The children got down on their hands and knees and went over the floor inch by inch.

"What about the furniture?" asked Bill. "Do we move that?"

"I guess we'll have to," said Jed.

"Can we do one piece at a time?" asked Liza. "Then if there's nothing there, we can move it back."

"All right," said Jed. "We'll do the bed first."

The children moved every piece of furniture in the room. But they found no loose boards, no hidden hinges, nothing that looked strange.

They had just moved the last piece of furniture back into place when Mom called, "I'm home. Is anybody hungry?"

"Starved!" yelled Bill. "I could eat a dozen sandwiches."

"Mind if I fix them one at a time?" asked Mom.

"Any old way," said Bill. "Just keep them coming."

16.
Punching Bricks

After lunch Jed said, "Did anybody have any ideas about finding the secret room?"

"Well, I think we should look over that floor in Liza's room again," said Bill. "We may have overlooked something."

"I was wondering about that brick wall in the basement," said Liza. "Do you think there might be a secret door there?"

"I never thought of that," said Jed.

"Maybe it just looks like a solid wall."

"Oh, no!" said Bill. "Don't tell me we're going to go around punching every brick in that wall."

"Can you think of another way to do it?" asked Jed.

Bill didn't answer for a minute. Then he said, "No, I guess you're right. Let's go start punching."

The children went to the basement.

"It sure looks solid enough," said Liza.

"Yeah," said Bill. "But you never can tell. Maybe we better divide it into three parts."

Jed did the dividing and soon the children were punching every brick in turn. They worked for a long time, but each brick was just a brick.

Finally Jed said, "I'm afraid there's nothing here."

"Well, for goodness sakes," said Bill, "can't we stop now?"

"We might as well," said Liza. "I've sure

had enough of this. Do you really think there's any use in going over the floor in my room again?"

"Do you have a better idea?" asked Jed.

"No," said Bill.

"Then it's that or give up. It won't hurt to have another look at that floor," said Jed. "It makes sense that the door should be there if it's not here."

"But please," said Bill, "let's take a little rest before we do that."

"I'm all for it," said Jed. "Liza, where are you going?"

"Just to my room," said Liza. "Come on in when you're ready to look again."

Liza was looking for her sneakers. She happened to glance out of the window and saw Mr. Hobbs.

"Boys," she called, "I have an idea."

"So let us in on it," said Bill.

"Mr. Hobbs," said Liza.

"What about Mr. Hobbs?" asked Jed.

"Well, he's been around for a long time," said Liza. "I bet he'd know if there was a secret room."

"Gee," said Bill, "he might know something at that."

"It's worth a try anyway," said Jed.

The children went into the yard.

"Mr. Hobbs," said Liza, "you've lived around here a long time, haven't you?"

"Born and raised in the house I'm living in now," said Mr. Hobbs.

"Then you know this house very well, don't you?" asked Jed.

"Sure do," said Mr. Hobbs. "Helped John Blake draw the plans and build it."

"You did?" said the children.

"That's right," said Mr. Hobbs.

"Then you would know if it has a secret room, wouldn't you?" asked Bill.

"Secret room!" said Mr. Hobbs. "What kind of nonsense are you talking now?"

"From the house plans it looks as if there should be a room beneath Liza's," said Jed.

"What house plans?" asked Mr. Hobbs.

"The ones we found in the attic," said Bill.

"Let me take a look at them," said Mr. Hobbs. "I can tell you if they belong to this house."

Jed went inside and got the house plans.

Mr. Hobbs took them and studied them for several minutes. Then he said, "Yep, these are the right plans."

"But see," said Jed, "there's a room under Liza's on that plan, but there's no room like that in the basement."

"It does look as if a room should be there," said Mr. Hobbs. "Now wait a minute and let me think back."

Mr. Hobbs began to weed a flower bed. He was silent so long the children thought he had forgotten them.

Then suddenly he said, "I remember now. John Blake was going to put a maid's room there. But he decided it was too damp, so that part of the cellar was never dug."

The children were too stunned to say anything.

"Secret room!" said Mr. Hobbs. "You children!"

He was still chuckling as the children walked away.

"Yeah, secret room," said Bill. "And after all that work."

17.
Flashing Lights

That night Liza lay on her bed waiting for sleep to come. It was a very dark night.

Suddenly two beams of light flashed across the room. Seconds later two more beams of light followed. Liza scooted out of bed.

"Jed! Bill!" she called, running to their room.

"What is it?" asked Jed.

"Gosh, you look like a ghost," said Bill. "Did you really see one?"

"No, at least I don't think so," said Liza. She was shaking.

"So calm down and tell us what's wrong," said Jed.

"Lights," said Liza. "Lights have been flashing in my room."

"Are you sure it wasn't moonlight?" asked Bill.

"There's no moon tonight," said Liza. "And besides, moonlight doesn't flash. This was two flashing lights."

"Where did they start?" asked Jed.

"They came through the window," said Liza.

"Did they do anything?" asked Bill. "I mean, like point to you?"

"No," said Liza. "They just flashed through the room and were gone in seconds."

"Come on," said Jed. "We'd better try to find out what this is."

The children went into Liza's room.

"Now where were you, Liza?" asked Jed.

"On my bed," said Liza.

"So we'll get on your bed," said Bill.

The children sat very quietly on Liza's bed. Nothing happened.

"Maybe the ghost knows we're all here," said Bill. "Maybe he only comes when there is one person."

"Well, he'll never come," said Jed, "if you don't keep quiet."

A few minutes later two lights flashed across the room. In seconds they were gone.

"Gosh," said Bill. "No wonder you were scared. Do you think the ghost will appear now?"

"He didn't before," said Liza. But the three children moved closer together.

A little later the lights flashed through the room again. When they had gone Jed said, "Okay, I'm going to find out what this is about."

"What are you going to do?" asked Bill.

"I'm going to hide behind the curtain. I want to see if I can tell where the lights are coming from," said Jed.

"Oh, do be careful," said Liza.

Jed slipped across the room. He hid himself behind the curtain where he could see outside. There were no flashing lights for several minutes.

"The ghost doesn't want Jed to see," said Bill.

Then all of a sudden lights flashed across the room again, and Jed began laughing. Oh, how he laughed!

"What is it?" asked Liza. "Jed, tell us what it is!"

"Are you having a fit or something?" asked Bill. "Tell us what it is."

"Gosh," said Jed. "We are stupid!"

"So we're stupid," said Bill. "But what about the lights?"

"They're car lights," said Jed. "When they come around that curve, they shine in Liza's room."

"Are you sure?" asked Liza.

"See for yourself," said Jed. "Here comes a car now."

And, sure enough, lights flashed across the room.

Then all three children began to giggle.

"Let's not tell Mom and Dad," said Liza. "They would think we had really lost our minds."

"Yeah," said Bill. "Imagine us being scared by car lights."

"Let's go to bed," said Jed. "Tomorrow's a big day."

18.
The Lucky Break

The children were almost too excited to eat breakfast the next morning. Everything went wrong.

Bill's elbow hit his glass of milk and turned it over on Liza.

"Oh, stop being so clumsy," said Liza.

And just as she said that she knocked over her orange juice.

"Now who's the clumsy one?" asked Bill.

Then they began to giggle. They just couldn't stop laughing.

Finally Mom said, "All right, children, that's quite enough. What on earth is wrong with you today?"

"It's nothing, Mom," said Jed. "We just want to get out and play."

"You'll clean up in here first," said Mom, "and the kittens must be fed."

"I'll do that now," said Jed.

"Liza, go and change your clothes and bring me those so I can soak them."

"Ahh, Mom," said Liza. "I'm not that wet."

"Run along, Liza," said Mom. "I'm at the end of my patience with you children this morning."

Finally Liza had changed her clothes and helped the boys clean up the kitchen. The children were free to go outside. They were in such a rush that they didn't even stop to

134

play with the kittens. They ran toward the hollow tree, Jed in the lead.

"It's here," he called.

"Oh, I'm so excited I can't wait," said Liza.

Jed pulled out a piece of paper and unfolded it.

"Another code!" he said.

He showed the paper to Liza and Bill. The paper read:

"ceyreneotstnn
ototetwdhaeo
moürihosifro"

"That looks even harder than the last one we had," said Bill.

"Does anybody have pencil and paper?" asked Jed.

"No," said Liza. "They're in my room."

The children went into Liza's room to try to solve the new puzzle. They tried everything they knew. They wrote it backward. They tried to unscramble the words. But nothing worked out. The puzzle remained unsolved.

"Gosh," said Liza, "at this rate we'll never know what the big surprise is."

"Yeah," said Jed. "This one has me stumped."

Bill continued to study the puzzle. Suddenly he said, "Just a minute now. I think I see it. Give me that pencil."

Bill began to write. When he got through it looked like this:

"cometoyourtreeinthewoodsthisafternoon."

"You've got it, Bill," said Jed. "I see it now."

"Sure," said Liza. "It's like Chinese writing. You have to read it downward."

"It says: 'come to your tree in the woods this afternoon,' " said Jed. "But how can we?"

"That's right," said Bill. "We're still being punished."

"And I won't go alone!" said Liza. "Maybe if I ask Dad to let you off he will," said Liza.

"But you won't see him until tonight," said Bill.

"Sure I will," said Liza. "Don't you remember? This is his afternoon off."

"That's right," said Jed. "Maybe if he won't let us off he'll go with us."

"That's a good idea," said Liza.

"Somehow we'll find a way to get to our tree," said Bill.

"But let's go outside now," said Jed.

The children stayed outside for a long while. They played with the kittens and tried to play ball. But they kept thinking about the message.

"I wonder what the big surprise is," said Bill. "This waiting is too much for me."

"I wonder who's leaving those clues," said Jed.

"Well, I say it's either Dad or old John Blake," said Bill.

"I still don't think a ghost would leave footprints," said Jed.

"But we have no proof that he wouldn't," said Bill.

"Those small footprints are what make me think it's not a ghost," said Liza.

"But who could have made them?" asked

Jed. "We have no close neighbors and there are no children that we know out here."

"I guess we'll have to wait until this afternoon to find out," said Bill.

"I wish Dad would hurry up and get home," said Jed.

"What are we going to do if he won't let us go or won't go with us?" asked Bill.

"If he says no," said Jed, "we'll know he's not the one, because if he left the clues he would want us to go."

"Then it would be all the more important to go," said Liza, "because it would mean somebody else was doing it."

"Oh, he's just *got* to let us go," said Jed.

"It must be getting close to lunchtime," said Bill.

"Let's go in," said Liza.

The children went into the kitchen. Mom was making piles of sandwiches.

"What's up, Mom?" asked Bill. "Why so many sandwiches?"

"It's such a beautiful day," said Mom. "I thought it would be nice to take a picnic lunch and go to the woods."

"The woods!" said the children.

"Sure," said Mom. "Can you think of a better place to have a picnic?"

"No," said Jed. "You just surprised us."

"A picnic is a great idea!" said Bill.

"Do you want us to do anything, Mom?" asked Liza.

"No," said Mom. "Just be ready when Dad gets here."

"Don't worry," said Bill. "We'll be ready."

"Let's go to our room," said Jed.

When they got there Bill said, "Now that's what you call a lucky break, Mom deciding on a picnic lunch today of all days."

"Yeah," said Jed. "I wonder what made her decide to do that?"

"Maybe she's in on this," said Bill, "with Dad."

"Yeah," said Jed. "Come to think of it, she didn't fuss very much when we brought home the kittens. Maybe she is in on it."

"It could be she just likes picnics," said Liza, "and it is a beautiful day."

"Well, we'll soon find out," said Bill. "I wish Dad would hurry."

19.
Mystery Untangled

As soon as Dad came home and changed his clothes, the family started for the woods. Liza, Bill, and Jed tried to wait for their parents, but they just could not do it.

Finally Jed said, "Is it all right if we run ahead?"

"Sure," said Dad. "We'll meet you at your tree."

When the children got to the tree they just stopped and stared.

"Golly, gee!" said Bill. "Look at that tree house!"

"That's the neatest one I've ever seen," said Jed.

"Come on, let's get in it!" said Liza.

The children scrambled up the ladder to the tree house just as Mom and Dad arrived.

Liza climbed down the ladder and hugged Dad.

"Thank you, thank you," she said.

"What am I being thanked for?" asked Dad.

"This tree house, Dad," said Bill. "It's the greatest."

"But I didn't build it," said Dad. "This is the first time I've seen it."

"You didn't!" said the children.

"Then who did?" asked Liza.

"Well," said Dad, "two of your very best friends had a lot to do with it."

"Our friends!" said Bill. "Who?"

Then the children heard giggling. They ran toward the sound. At the same time, two children burst out of the bushes.

"Mary! Jimmy!" said Liza. "What are you doing here?"

"Visiting our Uncle Dan," said Mary.

"But he doesn't live close to us," said Bill.

"No, he doesn't," said Jimmy, "if you go by the road. But if you cut through the woods, it's not far at all."

Then the children noticed the man who was with them.

"We didn't know that Mr. Dan Coleman was your Uncle Dan," said Jed.

"We called the other day to get you to play in the woods," said Mary. "But your mother said you were being punished. And we knew Liza wouldn't want to come without you."

The children looked at their mother.

"I didn't tell you," said Mom, "because I knew how disappointed you would be."

"But how did you know we wanted a tree house in this tree?" asked Jed.

"I can answer that," said Uncle Dan. "I was in the woods the first day you were here and I heard you say so. I was going to come over and introduce myself, but you left before I had finished the work I was doing."

"We have a tree house just like it on the other side of the fence," said Mary.

"When we knew you were being punished we asked Uncle Dan what we could do for you," said Jimmy.

"He told us about the tree house and said he would help us," said Mary. "He called your father to see if it would be all right."

"Dad, you knew all the time!" said Liza. "And you didn't give us a clue."

"You didn't ask for one," said Dad.

"Did you do all the puzzles, too?" asked Bill. "They were great."

"Uncle Dan helped us with those," said Mary. "We told him you liked mysteries and about the adventures you had at your grandparents' last summer."

"Uncle Dan suggested we give you another mystery to solve," said Jimmy.

"Well, you sure did that!" said Jed.

"We thought you would guess when you got the kittens, since we had promised to give you one," said Mary.

"But you said one, and there were three," said Liza.

"I know," said Mary. "But there were six in the litter and Uncle Dan only wanted to keep one. So Jimmy and I each took one and that left three for you."

"We did think about you when we got the kittens," said Jed. "But we had no idea you were anywhere around."

"Those puzzles were hard," said Jed, "but they were fun to figure out."

"What about the carvings?" asked Bill. "Where did they come from?"

"Actually, they were done by John Blake," said Uncle Dan. "He gave me a set when I was a little boy. I gave them to Mary and Jimmy and they wanted to share with you."

"We thought our ghost was doing all of it," said Bill.

"Well," said Uncle Dan, "in a way he was."

"What do you mean?" asked Jed.

"I guess I'm responsible for the house being thought haunted. It was like this. The first caretaker left because he was lonely on the job. He said he heard noises and wasn't comfortable there. The second caretaker, who was a very brash young fellow, went around bragging about how no haunted house would get the best of him. He'd get the ghost first. Somehow it just made me mad. So

I waited until he had been there for a couple of days, then one night I went over and rattled some chains and made a few weird noises. Well, you never saw anybody get out of a house so fast! He spread the word that the house was really haunted. So no one wanted to stay there. Then they gave the job to Jack Hobbs. He had his own house so he didn't live there. So you see, I guess I'm your ghost."

"Gee," said Bill, "I bet that was fun, scaring that boy away."

"You should know," said Liza. "You sure scared me that night."

"Who's hungry?" called Mom.

"We are," said the children.

"Well, come and help yourselves," said Mom. She had the lunch all spread out.

"Let's eat in the tree house," said Jed.

"Good idea," said Jimmy.

The children got their lunch and disap-

peared into the tree house. They only came out for second helpings.

After lunch they visited Mary and Jimmy's tree house. All afternoon they played in the woods.

That evening the children told Mom and Dad all about the old clock and how they had looked for a secret room. They showed them the puzzles they had solved. The children took turns telling the story.

When they had finished Dad said, "And you kept all that to yourselves! I kept waiting for you to tell us about the puzzles."

"Oh, no!" said Liza. "We couldn't. You see we thought it was either you or the ghost and we wanted to find out which one it was by ourselves."

"And now we found out it wasn't either one!" said Jed.

"We also found out the house isn't even haunted!" said Bill.

"But let's not tell," said Liza. "It would

spoil our party if anybody knew the house wasn't haunted. Agreed?"

"Agreed," said everyone.

"And you were the one who didn't want to live here because of the ghost," said Bill.

Liza grinned and said, "I just changed my mind."

"We better ask Mary and Jimmy not to tell," said Jed.

"Mr. Coleman said he would come to the party, too. Maybe he'll help us with the weird noises," said Liza.

"Gosh," said Jed, "we should start making invitations!"

"Just a minute," said Dad. "That can wait until tomorrow."

Mom said, "Right now—"

Bill interrupted. "Right now our mother is going to tell us to go take baths. Come on, kids."

Mom and Dad laughed as the children left the room.

Clues in the Woods
Who or what is taking the kitchen scraps from the garbage? Every night Grandma leaves table scraps in a wrapped plastic bag in the garbage can, where, according to plan, the McNellis children pick them up to feed their kittens. But one night the bag is taken, and the McNellis children don't have it. The twins, Liza and Bill, and brother Jed decide to find out what's going on. First the children discover Liza's missing red sweater in a part of the woods she hasn't been to before, next they read about runaway children in the newspaper, and then their new puppy is lost. The young detectives must put all the clues together and solve the mystery in the woods.

Key to the Treasure
Each summer Liza, Bill, and Jed visit their grandparents, and they hear the story of the sketches hung above the fireplace mantel. The sketches are clues to a hidden treasure, and no one has been able to figure them out for a century. There is a missing first clue, but when the children stumble upon the second clue, they're on their way. Could it be that on this visit they will solve the secret that has puzzled so many for more than a hundred years?

The Mystery of Hermit Dan
After a frightening run-in with Hermit Dan earlier in the summer, Liza, Bill, and Jed are determined to stay away from the old man. But the stories the islanders tell about him make them curious. Were Hermit Dan's ancestors really pirates? Why does he avoid people? What's in the box he keeps buried in the dunes? Liza, Bill, and Jed stir up plenty of excitement when they set out to discover the secrets of Hermit Dan's past.

The Ghosts of Cougar Island
Summer vacation is nearly over, and Liza, Bill, and Jed know it's almost time to leave their grandparents and the exciting adventures they've shared on Pirate Island. Before they head home, the trio is itching to solve the mystery of Cougar Island. But it's private property, and according to legend, trespassers will be haunted forever by the ghosts of the Cougar family. Ghosts or no ghosts, Liza, Bill, and Jed won't be satisfied until they've done some exploring.

Pirate Island Adventure
Summer vacation at Pirate Island! Liza, Bill, and Jed can't believe their grandparents' wonderful surprise. The excitement begins even before they reach the island, as Grandpa gives the first clue to the unsolved mystery of a long-lost family "treasure." Whether it's their frightening run-ins with Hermit Dan, a wild and scary romp with a swooping bat, or a midnight trip into the woods, tracking the series of weird picture clues leads the children all over the island and into all sorts of adventures.